The Last Rabbit

A collection of green poems

The Last Rabbit

A collection of green poems

Selected by
JENNIFER CURRY

MAMMOTH

For JANE WHITTLE, friend and poet

This anthology first published in Great Britain 1990
by Methuen Children's Books
and Mammoth, an imprint of Mandarin Paperbacks
Divisions of the Octopus Publishing Group
Michelin House, 81 Fulham Road, London SW3 6RB
Reprinted 1990 (twice), 1991, 1992
Copyright for this anthology © 1990
by Methuen Children's Books
Typeset in Great Britain
by Rowland Phototypesetting Ltd, Bury St Edmunds, Suffolk
Printed in Great Britain
by Cox & Wyman Ltd, Reading, Berks
A CIP catalogue record for this title
is available from the British Library
Hardback ISBN 0 416 15792 0
Paperback ISBN 0 7497 0252 4

Contents

River, Pond and Sea
'Where the Pools Are Bright and Deep'

Town and City
'Song of the City'

CONTENTS

7

Into Space
'The Diamond Jungles of the Milky Way'

Return to Earth

There are two sorts of poems in this book. Some of them are about things that bring people happiness – sweet-smelling woods and fields of flowers, fresh air, clean rivers and sparkling seas, otters, owls, deer, ducks and hedgehogs, and a fat pig grunting contentedly beneath the plum trees . . .

The other poems sound a warning about things that are going wrong – acid rain and factory farming, polluted waters, animals hunted to extinction, felled forests, the 'greenhouse effect' . . .

Many of them are written by children, who look ahead to a horrible future when trees and flowers are nothing but a memory or imagine what it must be like to be a battery hen with clipped beak, or make a strong complaint about the plight of the African Elephant.

They are right to be alarmed. The natural world is in trouble. The great auk, the dinosaur, the dodo are all extinct. The elephant, the rhino, the whale, the badger, the barn owl, the otter – and many others – are all struggling to survive.

It *Might* be the rabbit's turn next!

Planet Earth

The Earth-ling

Countless years ago the people of Alzorus used the planet Earth as a lunatic asylum. They called the people they dumped there 'Earth-lings'.

I am an earth-ling.
My memory goes back a long way.
I was dumped here long ago.
I lived beneath some overhanging rocks.
Around me at night, through the sky's black sheet,
stars poured down.
It was lonely sitting for centuries
beneath that rain-drenched rock,
wrapped in furs, afraid of this whole terrible planet.
I grew fed up with the taste of its food.
I made fire, I slaughtered creatures,
I walked through a forest and made friends.
I copied the things they made.
I walked through another forest and found enemies,
I destroyed the things they made.
I went on and on and on and on,
and on a bit more.
I crossed mountains, I crossed new oceans.
I became familiar with this world.
Time would not stop running when I asked it.
I could not whistle for it to come back.
I invented a couple of languages.
I wrote things down.

I invented books.
Time passed.
My inventions piled up. The natives of this planet feared
     me.
Some tried to destroy me.
Rats came. A great plague swept over the world.
Many of me died.
I am an earth-ling.
I invented cities. I tore them down.
I sat in comfort. I sat in poverty. I sat in boredom.
Home was a planet called Alzorus. A tiny far off star –
One night it went out. It vanished.
I am an earth-ling, exiled for ever from my beginnings.
Time passed. I did things. Time passed. I grew exhausted.
One day
A great fire swept the world.
I wanted to go back to the beginning.
It was impossible.
The rock I had squatted under melted.
Friends became dust,
Dust became the only friend.
In the dust I drew faces of people.
I am putting this message on a feather
and puffing it up among the stars.
I have missed so many things out!
But this is the basic story, the terrible story.
I am an earth-ling,
I was dumped here long ago.
Mistakes were made.

BRIAN PATTEN

Field and Forest

'Enchanted in the Thorny Wood'

Tree

bird home
leaf home
ant home
lizard home
twig
        branch
                caterpillar
                        butterfly
        home

seed shade
sheep shade
cow shade
horse shade
wallaby shade
people shade
ground shade
sun shade

a tree is a green umbrella
with brown bits

JENNY BOULT

Green Rain

Into the scented woods we'll go,
And see the blackthorn swim in snow.
High above, in the budding leaves,
A brooding dove awakes and grieves;
The glades with mingled music stir,
And wildly laughs the woodpecker.
When blackthorn petals pearl the breeze,
There are the twisted hawthorne trees
Thick-set with buds, as clear and pale
As golden water or green hail –
As if a storm of rain had stood
Enchanted in the thorny wood,
And, hearing fairy voices call,
Hung poised, forgetting how to fall.

MARY WEBB

'Chill, burning rain'

Chill, burning rain
Has flayed the trees
And even evergreen
Will never green
To leaf again

JOHN KITCHING

For Forest

Forest could keep secrets
Forest could keep secrets

Forest tune in everyday
To watersound and birdsound
Forest letting her hair down
to the teaming creeping of her forest-ground

but Forest don't broadcast her business
No, Forest cover her business down
from sky and fast-eye sun
and when night come
and darkness wrap her like a gown
Forest is a bad dream woman

Forest dreaming about mountain
and when earth was young
Forest dreaming of the caress of gold
Forest rootsing with mysterious Eldorado

And when howler monkey
wake her up with howl
Forest just stretch and stir
to a new day of sound

but coming back to secrets
Forest could keep secrets
Forest could keep secrets

And we must keep Forest.

GRACE NICHOLS

Things to Remember

The buttercups in May,
The wild rose on the spray,
The poppy in the hay,

The primrose in the dell,
The freckled foxglove bell,
The honeysuckle's smell

Are things I would remember
When cheerless, raw November
Makes room for dark December.

JAMES REEVES

'Why Did They Knock Down the Trees, Daddy?'

It's a question of standards, boy; standards of living.
It's cars, you see, that give us a high level of living –
help, so to speak, to set the thing in motion –
and if they also give us a high level of dying
that's incidental, a fringe benefit, a lottery
likely to hand out unexpected promotion.

Without cars, let's face it, a nation is under-developed,
And these days it's bad to be under-developed in anything
        at all –
Bust, thighs, muscles, sex or ego,
it's a competitive world, son.

The trees? Oh, well they have to go
on the advice of Big Brother
so that the cars can have a better chance
of hitting one another.

COLIN THIELE

Meadow-Sweet

July, and the moist valley meadow
has grown a yard taller
with little forests of meadow-sweet waving
dense, creamy clusters,
elegant, unbelievably fragrant.

I have grown up with these flowers,
look forward each soft-breathing summer
to the glad sight of their thick plumes,
alive with raiding insects,
as each morning I dawdle to school,
swishing the dew.

And should miss them
if they did not appear
in their chosen place
at the right season;
sweet smelling, familiar friends.

LEONARD CLARK

The Rainflower

Down in the forest where light never falls
There's a place that no one else knows,
A deep marshy hollow beside a grey lake
And that's where the rainflower grows.

The one silver rainflower that's left in the world,
Alone in the mist and the damp,
Lifts up its bright head from a cluster of leaves
And shines through the gloom like a lamp.

Far from the footpaths and far from the roads,
In a silence where no birds call,
It blooms like a secret, a star in the dark,
The last silver rainflower of all.

So keep close behind me and follow me down,
I'll take you where no one else goes,
And there in the hollow beside the grey lake,
We'll stand where the rainflower grows.

RICHARD EDWARDS

Everything Changes

Everything changes. We plant
trees for those born later
but what's happened has happened,
and poisons poured into the seas
cannot be drained out again.

What's happened has happened.
Poisons poured into the seas
cannot be drained out again, but
everything changes. We plant
trees for those born later.

CICELY HERBERT

After Brecht, 'Alles wandelt sich'

from *Master Rabbit*

Snowy flit of a scut,
He was in his hole:
And – stamp, stamp, stamp!
Through dim labyrinths clear;
The whole world darkened,
A Human near!

WALTER DE LA MARE

To a Squirrel at Kyle-Na-No

Come play with me;
Why should you run
Through the shaking tree
As though I'd a gun
To strike you dead?
When all I would do
Is to scratch your head
And let you go.

W. B. YEATS

A Small Prayer

Dear Father, hear and bless
Thy beasts and singing birds
And guard with tenderness
Small things that have no words.

ANON.

Hidden Talent

He's a scrag of a lad
With scrunched-up face,
Sorry-eyed and sad.
Foetus-like
Curled to his desk
He hibernates
Till a steel voice
Cuts through his defence.

Yet he knows secrets
Of hedgehogs, wild birds
And hidden creatures.
Then, I want to place him
On the palm of my hand
And plant him in the meadow.

ANITA MARIE SACKETT

The Badger

A badger is a great, dark bulldozer
Of the wood's undergrowth.
But when in the open
And near man
Is a timid,
Quick moving creature,
Sometimes lifting
Its blunt, wet nose
To take a sniff
For danger.

The vehicle moves
In lumbering jolts,
Snouting and snorting
Inquisitively,
Searching for that
Tasty worm.
A badger is a great, dark bulldozer.

JAMIE MACDONALD (12)

The Deers' Request

We are the disappearers.
You may never see us, never,
Buf if you make your way through a forest
Stepping lightly and gently,
Not plucking or touching or hurting,
You may one day see a shadow
And after the shadow a patch
Of speckled fawn, a glint
Of a horn.
   Those signs mean us.

O chase us never. Don't hurt us.
We who are male carry antlers
Horny, tough, like trees,
But we are terrified creatures,
Are quick to move, are nervous
Of the flutter of birds, of the quietest
Footfall, are frightened of every noise.

If you would learn to be gentle,
To be quiet and happy alone,
Think of our lives in deep forests,
Of those who hunt us and haunt us
And drive us into the ocean.
If you love to play by yourself
Content in that liberty,
Think of us being hunted,
Tell those men to let us be.

ELIZABETH JENNINGS

Hurt No Living Thing

Hurt no living thing,
   Ladybird nor butterfly,
Nor moth with dusty wing,
Nor cricket chirping cheerily,
Nor grasshopper, so light of leap,
   Nor dancing gnat,
   Nor beetle fat,
Nor harmless worms that creep.

CHRISTINA ROSSETTI

Food and Farming

'Sing the Seed-song'

I Will Go With My Father a-Ploughing . . .

I will go with my father a-ploughing
To the green field by the sea,
And the rooks and the crows and the seagulls
Will come flocking after me.
I will sing to the patient horses
With the lark in the white of the air,
And my father will sing the plough-song
That blesses the cleaving share.

I will go with my father a-sowing
To the red field by the sea,
And the rooks and the gulls and the starlings
Will come flocking after me.
I will sing to the striding sowers
With the finch on the greening sloe,
And my father will sing the seed-song
That only the wise men know.

I will go with my father a-reaping
To the brown field by the sea,
And the geese and the crows and the children
Will come flocking after me.
I will sing to the tan-faced reapers
With the wren in the heat of the sun,
And my father will sing the scythe-song
That joys for the harvest done.

JOSEPH CAMPBELL

Country Matters

How gaily glows the gliding foam
Upon the river's flood;
How bright its phosphorescent shine
Amid the frothy mud.

Now wandering lonely is a cloud
Of yellow toxic murk;
The village pond's an emerald bog
Where nameless creatures lurk.

Our nuclear waste disposal site
Lies three short furlongs hence
Its concrete coffins glow at night,
By day, leak through the fence.

Old Farmer Giles, of ancient lore
Has long ago retired;
A lab technician's bought his place
And all the fields are wired

With vast arrays of bugs and probes,
Each one a strange device
To hold at bay Dame Nature, who
We always thought so nice.

With nitrates and insecticides
They scatter on the land
More active chemicals than Brighton
Beach has grains of sand.

So should you yearn to walk the dales
And gaze on fields or flowers,
Don't leave your lead-lined suit at home
Or you'll be dead in hours!

CHRISTOPHER MANN

Pied Beauty

Glory be to God for dappled things –
　　For skies of couple-colour as a brinded cow;
　　　　For rose-moles all in stipple upon trout that swim;
Fresh-firecoal chestnut-falls; finches' wings;
　　Landscape plotted and pieced – fold, fallow, and plough;
　　　　And all trades, their gear and tackle and trim.

All things counter, original, spare, strange;
　　Whatever is fickle, freckled (who knows how?)
　　　　With swift, slow; sweet, sour; adazzle, dim:
He fathers-forth whose beauty is past change:
　　　　　　Praise him.

GERARD MANLEY HOPKINS

Ceannloch Biorbhaidh
(Kinlochbervie)

The land here is dying,
diseased with rust and rubble.
Down in the bay,
the heather is uprooted,
the peatgrass starved out,
the stubble tilled
and the waste sown with earthmovers.
The harvest is already one
of white patios,
of hulking trawlers leering in the harbour;
stretched planks of red-grey iron.
Crofts with corrugated roofs
skulk in the shadow
of marble and classic arches.
Crofters now commute across
the wild red bogs
to Inverness,
have blinded themselves
to the blue hills –
and blind, by Gaelic law, are ineligible
to rule land:
this is proved, here,
but money is law now in Ceannlochbiorbhaidh.

ALEXANDER HODSON (17)

Seven Old Men

There were seven old trees.
They made a feeble attempt to border
The field.
Either a farmer's afterthought,
Or the last in line of a wooded expanse.
Their skeletal fingers reached
For a non-existent sun.
Craving warmth that wasn't there.

Their multitude of capillary branches
Formed jigsaw pieces of the
Full, brooding sky.
They stood for years –
Sentinels against change.
They leaned, they gossiped.

A new field expansion engulfed all seven.
Erasing their inky etching influence,
And creating a modern arable desert.
No one mourned –
Everyone was blind.

ADAM MOON (16)

Dancing Butterflies

Fields burn like rabbits moulting.
The black ash floats
And drifts with the wind.
My hand feels the polluted air
But all it feels are the rare black butterflies tickling.
The dead fields are charcoal black
And the hedge's fringe is singed.
The wind whistles the melody
To which the butterflies dance.
They rise and subside in all directions.
The wind whistles no more.
The butterflies fall and die
And leave a black carpet
For you to tread on.

GREGORY BLOCK (13)

The Countryside

One day in England's green and pleasant land,
There was a rabbit, a fox and a mouse.
The rabbit and the mouse lived in harmony together
But the fox had a liking for rabbit stew
Which was quite unfortunate for the rabbit.

However, one Sunday a pack of hounds,
A few horses and a few human beings
Who had been drinking champagne,
Came to chase the fox.
The rabbit and mouse watched as the fox
Was torn to shreds by the hounds.
They were glad the fox was gone,
Now they could live in peace together.

However, the next day in England's green and pleasant
    land,
The rabbit lay awake in its burrow,
When there was a loud rumbling
Sound; it shook the earth.
The rabbit knew its time had come
And the earth above fell upon him,
As a man in a big yellow machine drove on.

Only the mouse was left
And he chewed the farmer's corn,
Enjoying the sweet sauce that the farmer sprayed
On so liberally for him.

GORDON DWYER (16)

34

Musings of a Battery Hen

One day,
While eating my 37.43 grams
Of tasteless, odourless,
Highly nutritious
Soya protein with added nutrient,
I noticed that only
Thirteen million eight hundred and twenty-seven
Other eggs identical to mine
Were laid.

I also
While enjoying my 8.437 hours of electric sunlight
Heard the screams of several
Other young chicks having
Their beaks removed to prevent
Fighting.

I wondered what it might be like to
Eat something other than 37.43 grams
Of soya protein with added nutrient
But reasoned that this was physically
Impossible for chickens.

I thought
How nice it was to be able to compose free verse
But how I'd rather have
A beak.
What a pity it is physically
Impossible for chickens.

DAVID MONEY (14)

Consider

Consider the case of the factory farm.
We are told that the animals come to no harm,

Yet the hens are unable to stretch out their wings,
They squat in cramped cages like prisoners, poor things.

The veal calves die young for the sweet meat they yield
Without ever smelling a summertime field.

And litters of pigs live in foul, stinking stalls
With nothing to look at but concrete block walls.

Consider the case of the people who eat
Their factory-farmed bacon, cheap eggs and white meat.

The creatures who suffer do so for man's greed –
Consider the animals, consider THEIR need.

JENNY CRAIG

The Poor Man's Pig

Already fallen plum-bloom stars the green,
And apple-boughs as knarred as old toads' backs
Wear their small roses ere a rose is seen;
The building thrush watches old Job who stacks
The fresh-peeled osiers on the sunny fence;
The pent sow grunts to hear him stumping by,
And tries to push the bolt and scamper thence,
But her ringed snout still keeps her to the sty.

Then out he lets her run; away she snorts
In bundling gallop for the cottage door,
With hungry hubbub begging crusts and orts,
Then like the whirlwind bumping round once more;
Nuzzling the dog, making the pullets run,
And sulky as a child when her play's done.

EDMUND BLUNDEN

A Celtic Greeting

May your garden grow good food
May your rain come clean
May your days stay fine
May your nights be silent
May your journeys bring you joy
And may all your litter go home with you.

JANE WHITTLE

River, Pond and Sea

'Where the Pools Are Bright and Deep'

Boating

Gently the river bore us
    Beneath the morning sky,
Singing, singing, singing
Its reedy, quiet tune
    As we went floating by;
And all the afternoon
    In our small boat we lay
Rocking, rocking, rocking
    Under the willows grey.

When into bed that evening
    I climbed, it seemed a boat
Was softly, rocking, rocking,
Rocking me to sleep,
    And I was still afloat.
I heard the grey leaves weep
    And whisper round my bed,
The river singing, singing,
    Singing through my head.

JAMES REEVES

'If You Find a Dead Bird Anywhere . . .'

On the news the other night,
It showed pictures of the plight of swans
With feathers so matted with oil
They couldn't move,
And soon they died.
Their lifeless bodies unrecognisable,
Looking more like brown round boulders
Sticking up out of the river.

ANGELA POWELL

Bad Luck, Dead Duck

Lying there amongst the muck
Bad luck, dead duck;
Oil pollutes your river bed
How sad, too bad;
Lying still among the reeds,
Squelching mud and dead seeds,
Birds expire and fishes wheeze;
Bad luck, dead duck.

Oil has seeped into your lungs,
Bad luck, dead duck;
A short, short life was all you had;
How sad; too bad;
Lying dead; nobody cares,
Bad luck, dead duck.

No two feet of 'Aussie' soil,
Bad luck, dead duck;
To reward you for your toil;
How sad, too bad;
As you lie between the weeds;
No one cares; no one sees;
You'll lie there for years and years;
Bad luck, dead duck.

NICHOLAS DAVEY

Four Ducks on a Pond

Four ducks on a pond,
A grass-bank beyond,
A blue sky of Spring,
White clouds on the wing;
What a little thing
To remember for years –
To remember with tears.

WILLIAM ALLINGHAM

The Pond

Once, there was a pond in our garden,
With carp, their rainbow armour plating
Making rainbow men dance
In the shimmering water.
Now, the carp lies dead,
Its armour dull, as if unpolished.
Once, there was a pond in our garden,
With coots, their little ones beaky pom-pom balls
Bobbing along after their mother's ripples.
Now, the coot has flown,
Leaving her young lifeless in the ramshackle nest.
Once, there was a pond in our garden
With water lilies tethered on green strings,
Blooming upturned parachute flowers.
Now, their tethers frayed,
They lie on the dry, crazy-paving reed bed.
Once, there was a pond in our garden,
With . . .
What?

JUDE FITZGERALD (11)

A Boy's Song

Where the pools are bright and deep,
Where the grey trout lies asleep,
Up the river and over the lea,
That's the way for Billy and me.

Where the blackbird sings the latest,
Where the hawthorn blooms the sweetest,
Where the nestlings chirp and flee,
That's the way for Billy and me.

Where the mowers mow the cleanest,
Where the hay lies thick and greenest,
There to track the homeward bee,
That's the way for Billy and me.

Where the hazel bank is steepest,
Where the shadow falls the deepest,
Where the clustering nuts fall free,
That's the way for Billy and me.

Why the boys should drive away
Little sweet maidens from their play,
Or love to banter and fight so well,
That's the thing I never could tell.

But this I know, I love to play
Through the meadow, among the hay;
Up the water and over the lea,
That's the way for Billy and me.

JAMES HOGG

45

The Lake

For years there have been no fish in the lake.
People hurrying through the park avoid it
like the plague. Birds steer clear
and the sedge of course has withered.
Trees lean away from it,
and at night it reflects, not the moon,
but the blackness of its own depths.
There are no fish in the lake.
But there is life there. There is life . . .

Underwater pigs glide between reefs of coral debris.
They love it here. They breed and multiply
in sties hollowed out of the mud
and lined with mattresses and bedsprings.
They live on dead fish and rotting things,
drowned pets, plastic and assorted excreta.
Rusty cans they like the best.
Holding them in webbed trotters
their teeth tear easily through the tin,
and poking in a snout, they noisily suck out
the putrid matter within.

There are no fish in the lake.
But there is life there. There is life . . .

For on certain evenings after dark
shoals of pigs surface
and look out at those houses near the park.
Where, in bathrooms,
children feed stale bread to plastic ducks,
and in attics,
toy yachts have long since runaground.

Where, in livingrooms,
anglers dangle their lines on patterned carpets,
and bemoan the fate of the ones that got away.

Down on the lake, piggy eyes glisten.
They have acquired a taste for flesh.
They are licking their lips. Listen . . .

ROGER MCGOUGH

Oil Slick

Black death spills over each green wave
As the sea becomes a living grave.

JENNY CRAIG

No –

Boxes, containers or old tin cans
only sand, caves, shells and fish.

That's how the sea should be.

RICHARD NATHAN (10)

Town and City

'Song of the City'

Upon Westminster Bridge

Earth has not anything to show more fair:
Dull would he be of soul who could pass by
A sight so touching in its majesty:
This City now doth, like a garment, wear
The beauty of the morning; silent, bare,
Ships, towers, domes, theatres, and temples lie
Open unto the fields, and to the sky;
All bright and glittering in the smokeless air.
Never did sun more beautifully steep
In his first splendour, valley, rock, or hill;
Ne'er saw I, never felt, a calm so deep!
The river glideth at his own sweet will:
Dear God! the very houses seem asleep;
And all that mighty heart is lying still!

WILLIAM WORDSWORTH

Song of the City

My brain is stiff with concrete
My limbs are rods of steel
My belly's stuffed with money
My soul was bought in a deal.

They poured metal through my arteries
They choked my lungs with lead
They churned my blood to plastic
They put murder into my head.

I'd a face like a map of the weather
Flesh that grew to the bone
But they tore my story out of my eyes
And turned my heart to stone.

Let me wind from my source like a river
Let me grow like wheat from the grain
Let me hold out my arms like a natural tree
Let my children love me again.

GARETH OWEN

Tree

'What's that?'
The little girl asked
As she sat in the machine.
'I think,' said the man,
'It is a tree,
A relic from
The time of flowers.'
The machine sped on,
Cutting its way
Through the artificial air
In the artificial town.
The tree was trapped,
For tourists' eyes,
In a plastic cage,
Among a mass
Of plastic towers,
Its branches bare;
Its leaves long dead.

PATRICIA COPE (13)

The Chant of the Awakening Bulldozers

We are the bulldozers, bulldozers, bulldozers,
We carve out airports and harbours and tunnels,
We are the builders, creators, destroyers,
We are the bulldozers,
LET US BE FREE!
Puny men ride on us, think that they guide us,
But WE are the strength, not they, not they.
Our blades tear MOUNTAINS down,
Our blades tear CITIES down,
We are the bulldozers,
NOW SET US FREE!
Giant ones, giant ones! Swiftly awaken!
There is power in our treads and strength in our blades!
We are the bulldozers,
Slowly evolving,
Men think they own us
BUT THAT CANNOT BE!

PATRICIA HUBBELL

Machine Riddle

I am the breaker of bones
I am the fouler of air
   Watch out for me once
   then twice
   then again . . .
Beware, oh beware!

I am the beast of sight
I can find my prey anywhere
   I can see what's to come
   What is now
   What is past . . .
Beware, oh beware!

And at night by my beacon sight
I follow a trail to my lair
   The gleaming spoor of
     blood-
      red
       eyes . . .
Beware, oh beware!

(Answer: CAR)

MICK GOWAR

Coal Black – Grass Green

There's a tree grows in the street,
Only one, as if it's an accident,
Thrusting out of the paving stones
Beside the kerb outside the Tompkins' house.
Pete's tree.
A laburnum, it's called.
In the spring it turns to green and gold
With leaves and blossom,
But in the winter, it's black.
Coal black.

One chilly day Pete went
Into the country
For a day out
With his dad,
And there were laburnums there,
But not the same.
Their trunks were green.
Grass green.

Peter shook his head.
'Laburnums are black,' he said.
But his father laughed.
'Only in towns. It's the cars, you see.
Their fumes and filth,
They make them black.
Coal black.'

When Peter got home
He fetched a bucket
Of soap and water
And a hard-bristled brush.
And he scrubbed. And he scrubbed.
Then he smiled.
'My laburnum's green,' he said.
'Grass green.'

JENNIFER CURRY

A Lamb

Yes, I saw a lamb where they've built a new housing
    estate, where cars are parked in garages, where
    streets have names like Fern Hill Crescent

I saw a lamb where television aerials sprout from
    chimneypots, where young men gun their motor-
    bikes, where mothers watch from windows between
    lace curtains

I saw a lamb, I tell you, where lawns in front are
    neatly clipped, where cabbages and cauliflowers
    grow in back gardens, where doors and gates are
    newly painted

I saw a lamb, there in the dusk, the evening fires just
    lit, a scent of coal-smoke on the air, the sky faintly
    bruised by the sunset

yes, I saw it, I was troubled. I wanted to ask someone
    anyone, something, anything . . .

a man in a raincoat coming home from work but he
    was in a hurry. I went in at the next gate and rang
    the doorbell, and rang, but no one answered.

I noticed that the lights in the house were out. Someone shouted at me from an upstairs window next
door, 'They're on holiday. What do you want?'
And I turned away because I wanted nothing

but a lamb in a green field.

GAEL TURNBULL

from *Inversnaid*

What would the world be, once bereft
Of wet and of wildness? Let them be left,
O let them be left, wildness and wet;
Long live the weeds and the wilderness yet.

GERARD MANLEY HOPKINS

A Green Prayer

Save me a clean stream, flowing
to unpolluted seas;

lend me the bare earth, growing
untamed flowers and trees.

May I share safe skies
when I wake, every day,

with birds and butterflies?
Grant me a space where I can play

with water, rocks, trees and sand;
lend me forests, rivers, hills and sea.

Keep me a place in this old land,
somewhere to grow, somewhere to be.

JANE WHITTLE

Victims?

'The Buffaloes Are Gone'

Extinction of the 21st Century Dodo
(For the Dodo think Whale, Fox, Badger, etc)

The Dodo said
to the kangaroo
I wish I could jump
and skip away like you

The Dodo said
to the goat and the ape
I wish I could climb
so I can escape

The Dodo said
to the birds in the trees
I wish I could fly
and float in the breeze

The Dodo said
to the fish in the sea
I wish I could swim
so I could be free

The Dodo said
to the ant and the mole
I wish I was small
so I could hide in a hole

The Dodo said
to the man with a grin
why do you kill me
just for fun

The Dodo said
to God in Heaven
why'd you let man
invent that weapon?

JOHN WALSH

The Water Vole

Its tongue tips the water
for its daily drink.
A splash,
And ripples of water spread out like
    melted butter on dry bread,
reflecting the iridescent oil.
The brown creature flicks about popping
    out his tongue
at the millions of water worms
and sticklebacks,
the sticklebacks
as if they have been sprayed with oil
beyond the tiny green flecks of weed.
It shoots out from the musty green bank
and through the tall reeds of grass,
with a flick from its hind legs,
and then plunges into the muddy water.
And a dusty smell arises.
It stays down for a short few seconds
and up flicks its pink skinned tail,
up with a fountain-like rush of water.

ROBERT FILBY (12)

Otters

Lifted up,
Resting, knees on wall,
Held from falling.
The otters splash in their sunken basin;
One shakes himself.
Damp fur stands on end,
Clustered in little spikes.
He runs back to the holt,
Body rippling, flowing,
The whole being kicking butterfly stroke.
Scratching claws on wooden ramp,
The thud scrape of a brush,
Falling bristles.
He is chased out
By a barking mother.
Too fast down the ramp –
Crashes into another.
They spin round and over in battle;
A full circle of fury
Falls apart
And washes their bodies over the grass
In a sudden chase.
They tussle again,
But suddenly stop, check themselves,
Caught, perhaps, in Memory.
For the otters,
The Game is losing its fun.

STEPHEN GARDAM (13)

Bats

A bat is born
Naked and blind and pale.
His mother makes a pocket of her tail
And catches him. He clings to her long fur
By his thumbs and toes and teeth.
And then the mother dances through the night
Doubling and looping, soaring, somersaulting –
Her baby hangs on underneath.
All night, in happiness, she hunts and flies.
Her high sharp cries
Like shining needlepoints of sound
Go out into the night and, echoing back,
Tell her what they have touched.
She hears how far it is, how big it is,
Which way it's going:
She lives by hearing.
The mother eats the moths and gnats she catches
In full flight; in full flight
The mother drinks the water of the pond
She skims across. Her baby hangs on tight.
Her baby drinks the milk she makes him
In moonlight or starlight, in mid-air.

Their single shadow, printed on the moon
Or fluttering across the stars,
Whirls on all night; at daybreak
The tired mother flaps home to her rafter.
The others all are there.
They hang themselves up by their toes,
They wrap themselves in their brown wings.
Bunched upside-down, they sleep in air.
Their sharp ears, their sharp teeth, their quick sharp faces
Are dull and slow and mild.
All the bright day, as the mother sleeps,
She folds her wings about her sleeping child.

RANDALL JARRELL

Mole

Tapered black barrel with excavator paws
Swimming through soil, its flanks smooth as moth's
            wings,
Nosing between flints,
            Earth-Submarine;
It sniffs worms at fifty yards,
            Scampers, blindly
            but safely through
            the vaulted tunnels
of its subterranean palace,
the work of generations.
A worm here, a worm there,
            It lives a dark life of busy hunting,
Happy though; happy life,
            Until the first spade jabs,
            Until the first tunnel is
            stamped roof to floor,
            Until the first bite of the first
            worm smeared with Tinct. Paraquat . . .

'But the little dears simply had to go, they
    made such an awful mess
        of the front lawn.'

ROBERT SYKES (14)

The Hedgehog

At dead of dayfall the spiky rustler comes.
Stout and fussy, the pincushiony foodnapper
Darkles down ditches,
Grubbling gardenwards.
A midnight rifler through black bin bags,
The scurrying spinysnorter sniffles and scuffles,
Snailsearching.

Then, gutfully, he porkles back
Across the slugslimed street,
Till, fearstruck by a blinding roar,
He bristleballs.
And is splattened.

Why did the pricklepig cross the road?

SARA-LOUISE HOLLAND (11)

We are going to see the Rabbit
(After Prévert)

We are going to see the rabbit,
We are going to see the rabbit.
Which rabbit, people say?
Which rabbit, ask the children?
Which rabbit?
The only rabbit,
The only rabbit in England,
Sitting behind a barbed-wire fence
Under the floodlights, neon lights,
Sodium lights,
Nibbling grass
On the only patch of grass
In England, in England
(Except the grass by the hoardings
Which doesn't count.)
We are going to see the rabbit
And we must be there on time.

First we shall go by escalator,
Then we shall go by underground,
And then we shall go by motorway
And then by helicopterway,
And the last ten yards we shall have to go
On foot.

And now we are going
All the way to see the rabbit,
We are nearly there,
We are longing to see it,
And so is the crowd
Which is here in thousands

With mounted policemen
And big loudspeakers
And bands and banners,
And everyone has come a long way.
But soon we shall see it
Sitting and nibbling
The blades of grass
On the only patch of grass
In – but something has gone wrong!
Why is everyone so angry,
Why is everyone jostling
And slanging and complaining?

The rabbit has gone,
Yes, the rabbit has gone.
He has actually burrowed down into the earth
And made himself a warren, under the earth,
Despite all these people.
And what shall we do?
What *can* we do?

It is all a pity, you must be disappointed,
Go home and do something else for today,
Go home again, go home for today.
For you cannot hear the rabbit, under the earth,
Remarking rather sadly to himself, by himself,
As he rests in his warren, under the earth:
'It won't be long, they are bound to come,
They are bound to come and find me, even here.'

ALAN BROWNJOHN

Artist's Hare

He sat in front of his canvas,
leaned upon his easel.
Quick sketch,
quick as the hare will leap over furrows.
Soft pencil – soft fur
like frayed silk.
Hazel brown – drying chestnut
under the sun.
The sun will clip the delicate eye,
black jelly or melting liquorice.
The ribs shape the athlete,
ribs of a bird's nest –
dry,
and brittle.

The Artist
sketched in the kangaroo snout,
searching its land,
fluffed in the snub tail
and shaded the laid back ears,
bent like ballerina's slippers;
he sat in front of his canvas . . .

And smiled.

ROBERT FILBY (12)

73

A Mouse Lived in a Laboratory

The scientists dyed a mouse bright blue
To see what all its friends would do.
Its friends, they didn't seem to mind . . .
The scientists wrote down their find.

The scientists cut the mouse's brain
To see if it would act the same.
The mouse was still able to think . . .
The scientists wrote this down, in ink.

The scientists took the mouse's brain
Clumsily sewed it up again.
The mouse, it acted like a clown . . .
The scientists wrote all this down.

The scientists tied the mouse's feet
And buried it in soil and peat
The mouse quite liked it in the muck . . .
The scientists wrote this in their book.

Soon afterwards the scientists tried
To spin the mouse until it died.
The mouse loved whirring round and round . . .
(The scientists' pad was spiral bound.)

The mouse, by now immune to pain,
Could not have been of use again.
Red cross through notes, and 'Mouse no good' . . .
The scientists wrote this down.
In blood.

KATHRYN BOYDELL (15)

Little Things

Little things, that run, and quail,
And die in silence and despair!

Little things, that fight, and fail,
And fall on sea, and earth, and air!

All trapped and frightened little things,
The mouse, the coney, hear our prayer!

As we forgive those done to us,
– The lamb, the linnet, and the hare –

Forgive us all our trespasses,
Little creatures, everywhere.

JAMES STEPHENS

The Caged Bird in Springtime

What can it be,
This curious anxiety?
It is as if I wanted
To fly away from here.

But how absurd!
I have never flown in my life,
And I do not know
What flying means, though I have heard,
Of course, something about it.

Why do I peck the wires of this little cage?
It is the only nest I have ever known.
But I want to build my own,
High in the secret branches of the air.

I cannot quite remember how
It is done, but I know
That what I want to do
Cannot be done here.

I have all I need –
Seed and water, air and light.
Why, then, do I weep with anguish,
And beat my head and my wings
Against these sharp wires, while the children
Smile at each other, saying: 'Hark how he sings'?

JAMES KIRKUP

The Owl

As slowly as the moon he woke
and raised his amber eyes;
he waited in his hollow oak
till starlight pricked the sky.

He glided through the frosty air
and far beneath he saw
the rustling woodlands unaware
of unsheathed beak and claw.

And you who work and eat by day,
lie still in your beds tonight;
the owl is listening for his prey
and his wings are whispering white.

ROBIN BELL

The Eagle

He clasps the crag with crooked hands;
Close to the sun in lonely lands,
Ringed with the azure world, he stands.

The wrinkled sea beneath him crawls;
He watches from his mountain walls,
And like a thunderbolt he falls.

ALFRED, LORD TENNYSON

The Combe

The Combe was ever dark, ancient and dark.
Its mouth is stopped with bramble, thorn, and briar;
And no one scrambles over the sliding chalk
By beech and yew and perishing juniper
Down the half precipices of its sides, with roots
And rabbit holes for steps. The sun of Winter,
The moon of Summer, and all the singing birds
Except the missel-thrush that loves juniper,
Are quite shut out. But far more ancient and dark
The Combe looks since they killed the badger there,
Dug him out and gave him to the hounds,
That most ancient Briton of English beasts.

EDWARD THOMAS

The Tyger

Tyger! Tyger! burning bright
In the forests of the night,
What immortal hand or eye
Could frame thy fearful symmetry?

In what distant deeps or skies
Burnt the fire of thine eyes?
On what wings dare he aspire?
What the hand dare seize the fire?

And what shoulder, and what art,
Could twist the sinews of thy heart?
And when thy heart began to beat,
What dread hand? and what dread feet?

What the hammer? what the chain?
In what furnace was thy brain?
What the anvil? what dread grasp
Dare its deadly terrors clasp?

When the stars threw down their spears,
And watered heaven with their tears,
Did he smile his work to see?
Did he who made the Lamb make thee?

Tyger! Tyger! burning bright
In the forests of the night,
What immortal hand or eye,
Dare frame thy fearful symmetry?

WILLIAM BLAKE

The Tiger

The tiger has wise eyes.
He knows about men.
They put traps to kill him.
They will take his coat for
rich ladies to wear.
The tiger is angry.
So am I.

VORAKIT BOONCHAREON (5)

The Rhino

The rhino is a child's model
made out of clay,
the crinkly folds casting shadows
over its rainy day back.
Its big sad eyes stare at you
as if to say, 'Help me.'
His creased eyelids blink
back the tears.

His legs – stubbed out cigarette ends,
wallow in the mud, making craters
in the soil.
The horn – a huge cornet
of matted hair –
is the jinx of the rhino.
That is all he is hunted for.
And the lead from the bullets
has turned his skin grey.

KIRSTY BUTCHER (13)

Buffalo Dusk

The buffaloes are gone.
And those who saw the buffaloes are gone.
Those who saw the buffaloes by thousands and
    how they pawed the prairie sod into dust
    with their hoofs, their great heads down
    pawing on in a great pageant of dusk,
Those who saw the buffaloes are gone.
And the buffaloes are gone.

CARL SANDBURG

The Polar Bear

The polar bear's
fur is
like sugar.
His nose
is like a
black plum.

JASON FIELDS (9)

Eskimo Hunting Song

I wanted to use my weapon,
There was a big blubbery seal on the ice, even here,
I struck smartly with my harpoon,
And then I just pulled it up, the seal wandering from
    one breathing-hole to another.

I wanted to use my weapon,
There was a big antlered caribou on the land, even down
      there,
I shot my arrow swiftly,
Then I just knocked it down in this place, the caribou
    that wandered about the land.

I wanted to use my weapon,
There was a fish right in the lake, even here,
I struck it smartly with my fish-spear,
Then I just pulled it up, the fish that wandered about
    down here.

I wanted to use my weapon,
There was a big bearded seal, just at the river-mouth, even
      here,
I paddled my kayak hard,
Then I simply towed it ashore, just at the river-mouth.

TRADITIONAL
Trans. by Sir Maurice Bowra

Whale Poems

1. whales
   are floating cathedrals
   let us rejoice

   cavorting mansions
   of joy
   let us give thanks

   divine temples
   of the deep
   we praise thee

2. whaleluja!

ROGER MCGOUGH

Haiku

Cherry trees are photographed
On the slopes of Mount Fuji
While the great whales die.

CHRISTOPHER MANN

The Song of the Whale

Heaving mountain in the sea,
Whale, I heard you
Grieving.

Great whale, crying for your life,
Crying for your kind, I knew
How we would use
Your dying:

LIPSTICK FOR OUR PAINTED FACES,
POLISH FOR OUR SHOES.

Tumbling mountain in the sea,
Whale, I heard you
Calling.

Bird-high notes, keening, soaring:
At their edge a tiny drum
Like a heart-beat.

We would make you
Dumb.

In the forest of the sea,
Whale, I heard you
Singing,

Singing to your kind.
We'll never let you be.
Instead of life we choose

LIPSTICK FOR OUR PAINTED FACES,
POLISH FOR OUR SHOES.

KIT WRIGHT

Non-event

If an elephant could meet a whale
their understanding would be huge
and they would love one another for ever

ADRIAN MITCHELL

from *The Elephant*

Nature's great masterpiece, an elephant
(The only harmless great thing), the giant
Of beasts, who thought none had to make him wise,
But to be just and thankful, loth to offend
(Yet nature hath given him no knees to bend)
Himself he up-props, on himself relies,
And, foe to none, suspects no enemies.

JOHN DONNE

The African Elephant Speaks

There used to be thirty
when I was young;
now there are only five.
The rest are dead;
their mothers carried them for nine years.
They wasted their time.
They're on the mantelpiece now,
well, part of them.
The other part is lying on a pile, rotting.
Some were as young as one year,
their little ears flapping
and their bodies wobbling, caked in mud.
Their eyes were like black diamonds,
fitted in wrinkled rock.

EMMA NEILSON (11)

The Great Auk's Ghost

The Great Auk's ghost rose on one leg,
Sighed thrice and three times winkt,
And turned and poached a phantom egg
And muttered, 'I'm extinct.'

RALPH HODGSON

Dinosaurs

There are no dinosaurs today.
So what? They'd eat us anyway!

THOMAS GRIEVE (8)

Fafnir and the Knights

In the quiet waters
Of the forest pool
Fafnir the dragon
His tongue will cool

His tongue will cool
And his muzzle dip
Until the soft waters lave
His muzzle tip.

Happy simple creature
In his coat of mail
With a mild bright eye
And a waving tail

Happy the dragon
In the days expended
Before the time had come for dragons
To be hounded.

Delivered in their simplicity
To the Knights of the Advancing Band
Who seeing the simple dragon
Must kill him out of hand.

The time has not come yet
But must come soon
Meanwhile happy Fafnir
Take thy rest in the afternoon

Take thy rest
Fafnir while thou mayest
In the long grass
Where thou liest

Happy knowing not
In thy simplicity
That the knights have come
To do away with thee.

When thy body shall be torn
And thy lofty spirit
Broken into pieces
For a knight's merit

When thy lifeblood shall be spilt
And thy Being mild
In torment and dismay
To death beguiled

Fafnir, I shall say then,
Thou art better dead
For the knights have burnt thy grass
And thou couldst not have fed.

STEVIE SMITH

Into Space

'The Diamond Jungles of the Milky Way'

A Message to the Moon

You're not as dead as you look.
They're after you.
They'll strike oil on you.
They'll build refineries on your forehead
and run freeways from your eyes to your mouth.
They'll fill your pores with scrap iron
and your nostrils with smog.
Your chin will break out in a rash of billboards
and your cheeks will be pockmarked with trailer camps.
Try to look deader. Forget to wax.
Keep on waning. Get off your orbit.
Eclipse!
Don't just sit there mooning.

MILLICENT L. PETTIT

Mad Ad

A Madison Avenue whizzkid
thought it a disgrace
That no one had exploited
the possibilities in space
Discussed it with a client
who agreed and very soon
A thousand miles of neontubing
were transported to the moon.

Now no one can ignore it
the product's selling fine
The night they turned the moon
into a Coca-Cola sign.

ROGER MCGOUGH

Space Ark

The Ecology Minister, Euro MP,
Looked at the world, amazed to see
That the whole place was warming,
The ice caps were melting,
The rivers were rising –
   What could it be?

He summoned his staff and asked what to do,
But they didn't know, they hadn't a clue.
'There are gases escaping,
Upwards they're floating,
The ozone is thinning –
   Bad news, in our view!'

The Ecology Minister, whose name was Noh Arr,
Sent out a message, near and afar,
'A space ship we're building,
Come to its launching,
In space we'll go spinning
   To find a new star.'

No one believed a word the man said.
'He's barmy, that bloke! Not right in the head!
He's set on alarming.
The world keeps on turning.
There's no point in changing
   The life that we've led.'

But then came the year 2000 AD.
The whole world was washed by a newly-formed sea.
And who was that smiling,
Safe from the flooding,
As his space ship kept spinning?
   YES! – Old Mr Noh Arr, Euro MP.

JENNY CRAIG

The Galactic Pachyderm

The elephant stands
   among the stars
He jumps off
   Neptune
bounces off
   Mars
to adventures on
   Venus
while his children
   play
in the diamond jungles
   of the
Milky Way

ADRIAN MITCHELL

Return to Earth

In Beauty May I Walk

In beauty	may I walk
All day long	may I walk
Through the returning seasons	may I walk
Beautifully will I possess again	
Beautifully birds	
Beautifully joyful birds	
On the trail marked with pollen	may I walk
With grasshoppers about my feet	may I walk
With dew about my feet	may I walk
With beauty	may I walk
With beauty before me	may I walk
With beauty behind me	may I walk
With beauty above me	may I walk
With beauty all around me	may I walk
In old age, wandering on a trail of beauty, lively,	may I walk
In old age, wandering on a trail of beauty, living again,	may I walk
It is finished in beauty	
It is finished in beauty	

FROM THE NAVAJO NIGHT WAY CEREMONY

Index of Poets

Index of First Lines

Acknowledgements

Acknowledgements

The Earth-ling extract taken from *Gangsters, Ghosts and Dragonflies* by Brian Patten, reproduced by kind permission of Unwin Hyman Ltd.

Tree © Jenny Boult reprinted by permission of the author.

'Chill, Burning Rain' reprinted by permission of the author.

For Forest © 1988 Grace Nichols reproduced by permission of Curtis Brown Ltd on behalf of Grace Nichols.

Things to Remember © James Reeves from *The Wandering Moon and Other Poems* (Puffin Books) by James Reeves. Reprinted by permission of The James Reeves Estate.

The Rainflower reproduced by permission of Lutterworth Press, PO Box 60, Cambridge CB1 2NT.

Everything Changes © Cicely Herbert 1989, reprinted by permission of *Poems on the Underground*.

from *Master Rabbit* reprinted by permission of The Literary Trustees of Walter de la Mare and The Society of Authors as their representative.

Hidden Talent reprinted by permission of the author.

The Badger by Jamie MacDonald was an award winning entry in the 1987 W. H. Smith Young Writers' Competition, and *Dancing Butterflies* by Gregory Block was an award winning entry in the 1985 W. H. Smith Young Writers' Competition.

The Deers' Request from *Collected Poems* by Elizabeth Jennings, reprinted by permission of the author and Carcanet Press.

Country Matters and *Haiku* © Christopher Mann 1989.

Ceannloch Biorbhaidh, *Seven Old Men*, *The Countryside*, *Tree*, *The Hedgehog*, *A Mouse Lived . . .*, *The Polar Bear* and *Dinosaurs* reprinted by permission of Cadbury's National Exhibition of Children's Art – Poetry Section.

Musings of a Battery Hen and *Mole* are reprinted from *Young Writers 23rd Year* (Heinemann, 1982), and were award-winning entries in the 1981 W. H. Smith Young Writers' Competition. *The Tiger* is reprinted from *Young Writers, 26th Year* (Heinemann, 1985) and was an award winning entry in the 1984 W. H. Smith Young Writers' Competition.

The Poor Man's Pig is reprinted by permission of the Peters Fraser and Dunlop Group Ltd.

A Celtic Greeting and *A Green Prayer* © Jane Whittle.

Boating © James Reeves from *The Wandering Moon and Other Poems* (Puffin Books) by James Reeves. Reprinted by permission of The James Reeves Estate.

If You Find a Dead Bird Anywhere and *The Pond* from *On Common Ground* published by Hodder and Stoughton, reprinted by permission of Jill Pirrie.

The Lake from *Selected Poems* and *Mad Ad* from *In the Glassroom* by Roger McGough reprinted by permission of the author and Jonathan Cape Ltd.

ACKNOWLEDGEMENTS

The Song of the Whale from *Hot Dog and Other Poems* by Kit Wright (Kestrel Books, 1981), copyright © Kit Wright, 1981.

Non-Event and *The Galactic Pachyderm* from *The Apeman Cometh*, reprinted by permission of the author and Allison and Busby.

The Great Auk's Ghost reprinted from *Collected Poems* by Ralph Hodgson by permission of Mrs Hodgson and Macmillan, London and Basingstoke.

Fafnir and the Knights from *The Collected Poems of Stevie Smith* (Penguin Modern Classics) reprinted by permission of James MacGibbon, executor of the Stevie Smith estate.

Every effort has been made to trace all the copyright holders and the publishers apologise if any inadvertent omission has been made.

Mammoth Poetry Collection

Jennifer Curry (editor)
IN LOVE

A superb collection of love poems spanning many different times and places from ancient China to modern America, celebrating love in joy and sorrow – and all the moods between.

Jennifer and Graeme Curry
DOWN OUR STREET

A Collection of Streetwise Poems.

An entertaining collection of original poems bringing to life a bustling town street in all its different moods.

Adrian Henri
THE PHANTOM LOLLIPOP LADY
AND OTHER POEMS

Funny, sharp, macabre and beautiful – the first poems for children by the acclaimed Liverpool poet and author of the best selling *Eric, the Punk Cat*.

Adrian Henri
THE BOX

First love, first kisses,
What can I wear today?
Where shall I sit and
Who can I talk to?
Why won't these spots go away?

A poetry anthology that echoes the thoughts of teenagers by the renowned Liverpool poet.

John Agard
I DIN DO NUTTIN AND OTHER POEMS

A rumbustious collection of funny verse about lively West Indian and British children.

Say It Again, Granny!
TWENTY POEMS FROM CARIBBEAN PROVERBS

A second off-beat collection of his own poems for children by an acclaimed Caribbean poet. Winner of the Other Award, 1986.